Deinonychus
'Terrible Claw'

Zephyrosaurus
'Zephyr's Lizard'

Tenontosaurus
'Tendon Lizard'

Move to the back of the book for more dinosaurs.

DINOSAUR IN DANGER

Paul Geraghty

HUTCHINSON

London   Sydney   Auckland   Johannesburg

Beneath the great volcano, eerie
whoops echoed from the forest.
Far in the valley, a rusty voice
roared back. Something rustled in
the trees and a shriek of startled
pterosaurs took to the sky.
It was dawn in Laurasia.

Talon, a young deinonychus, burst from
the bushes to watch them fly.

Just then, a dragonfly dipped by and she sprang after it. Her tail whipped the ferns as she swerved and skipped. The playful chase took her further away from the rest of her pack.

Then the ground shuddered. Talon stopped, alarmed.
With a mighty blast the great volcano burst into the sky.
She looked up, terrified, as snakes of lava raced down
the mountain. Soon the forest all around was leaping
with flames.

Talon fled from the fire, but the rest of her pack had run the other way.

She sheltered from the fury of the heat in a stony stream as the fire raged all around.

When the last flames finally died, Talon set off in search of her family. Alone and afraid, she called out but no one called back. Nothing moved.

The land lay dark, silent and deserted.

It took days of travel for Talon to find life again,
and each day she grew hungrier.

With the rest of her pack she could tackle
big dinosaurs, but alone she had no chance.
The smaller ones were all too quick for her,
so she snapped at insects and tiny mammals
instead. And when she did catch something it
was never enough.

Talon searched the forest for food.
She smelled meat! Two terrifying carnosaurs
had made a kill. Very carefully she crept closer.
A twig cracked behind her . . .

. . . and a giant mouth snapped at her tail!

Talon screamed and leapt away.

She felt the creature's hot breath
as she ran. She ran until she knew
she was safe, but still she kept on.
She ran until her throat was raw.
Then, still shaking, she curled up
but was too hungry to sleep.

Next morning, Talon
was stirred by a familiar sound.
A pack of deinonychus, just like her!
She ran to meet them, calling as she went, but
in the clearing she stopped. It was the coastal pack;
her old enemies. They turned on her and chased her away.

Although the pack was hostile, Talon stayed nearby. It was better than being alone. And when they hunted she could eat their leftovers.

She watched as they played in the sun and prepared to hunt. The air was electric as they jumped and nipped and yelped, just as her own family had done. She wished that she could join in too.

Then came a signal and the pack trotted off towards a herd of iguanodon. Nervously the great plant eaters stamped and turned, making purple mooing noises.

The hefty creatures started to run. Then they panicked and began to stampede.

One iguanodon broke away from the rest and
the pack took chase. Now they were sprinting.
Talon's heart kicked wildly as she watched,
thinking, Food! Food! Food! with every beat.
    Then the great beast swerved and headed
straight for her.

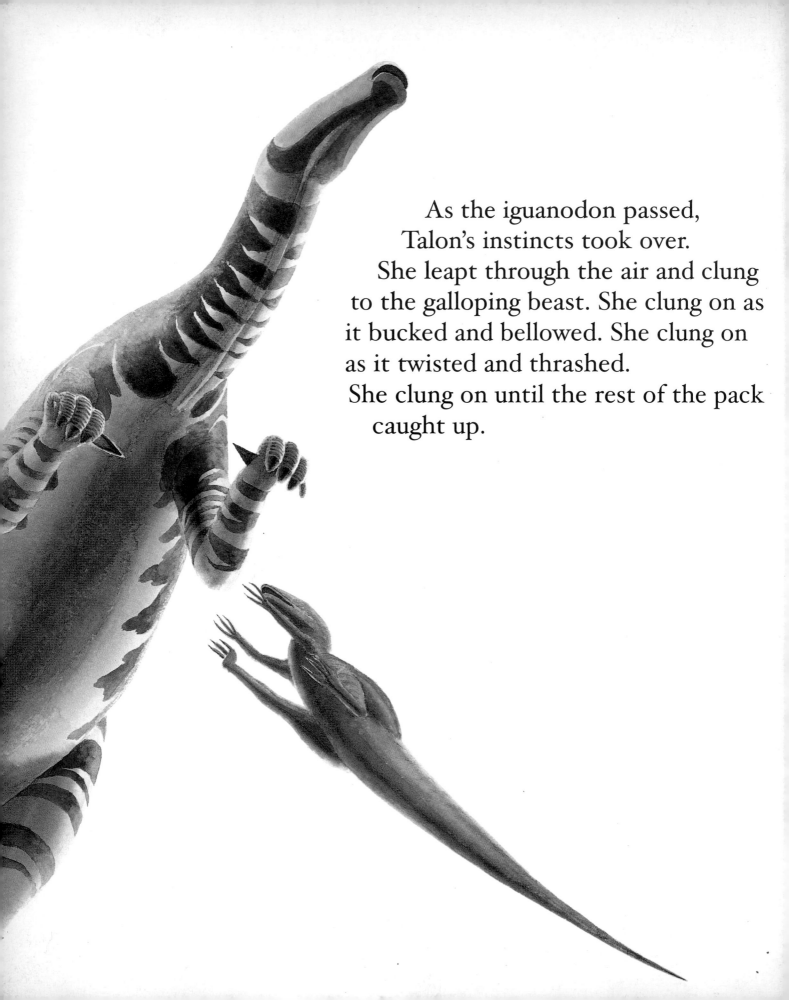

As the iguanodon passed,
Talon's instincts took over.
She leapt through the air and clung
to the galloping beast. She clung on as
it bucked and bellowed. She clung on
as it twisted and thrashed.
She clung on until the rest of the pack
caught up.

As usual, Talon was chased from the feast, but this time not quite as far as before. The pack had seen she was a good hunter and let her wait nearby as they ate. Then she was allowed her share. And for the first time since the great fire, she had a proper meal.

Like a constant shadow, Talon continued to follow the pack. And when one of their babies, who had wandered too far, was snatched by a utahraptor, only she heard its cries. Talon called out in alarm. The whole pack looked back as the slavering killer opened its jaws.

Bravely, Talon screamed and lunged.

Startled, the raptor dropped the baby, then fled as the whole pack poured over the bank to help. The youngster scampered back to the group, shaken but unharmed.

And Talon joined them too. This time, no one chased her away. Instead they bumped and nuzzled her like an old friend. She was part of a family again.

That night, as the moon rose over Laurasia, Talon ran with the pack for the first time.

And from then on, she hunted and played and tumbled and teased with the rest of them until no one could remember that she had ever been a stranger.

For Gabby, Daw
and dinosaur dreamers everywhere

Special thanks to Dr Norman Macleod,
keeper of palaeontology at the Natural History Museum, London,
for his invaluable help with research

DINOSAUR IN DANGER
A HUTCHINSON BOOK 0 09 188483 7

Published in Great Britain by Hutchinson,
an imprint of Random House Children's Books

This edition published 2004

1 3 5 7 9 10 8 6 4 2

RANDOM HOUSE CHILDREN'S BOOKS
61–63 Uxbridge Road, London W5 5SA
A division of The Random House Group Ltd

RANDOM HOUSE AUSTRALIA (PTY) LTD
20 Alfred Street, Milsons Point, Sydney,
New South Wales 2061, Australia

RANDOM HOUSE NEW ZEALAND LTD
18 Poland Road, Glenfield, Auckland 10, New Zealand

RANDOM HOUSE (PTY) LTD
Endulini, 5A Jubilee Road, Parktown 2193, South Africa

THE RANDOM HOUSE GROUP Limited Reg. No. 954009
www.kidsatrandomhouse.co.uk
www.paulgeraghty.net

A CIP catalogue record for this book is available from the British Library.

Printed in Hong Kong

Pleurocoelus
'Hollow Side'

Acrocanthosaurus
'High Spine Lizard'

Sauropelta
'Lizard Shield'